ASTRID & APOLLO

AND THE
MAGIC PEPPER

BY
V.T. BIDANIA

ILLUSTRATED BY
EVELT YANAIT

PICT

To my mom, who took us gardening —VTB

Astrid and Apollo is published by Picture Window Books,
an imprint of Capstone.
1710 Roe Crest Drive
North Mankato, Minnesota 56003
capstonepub.com

Library of Congress Cataloging-in-Publication Data
Names: Bidania, V.T., author. | Yanait, Evelt, illustrator.
Title: Astrid and Apollo and the magic pepper / by V.T. Bidania ; illustrated by Evelt Yanait.
Description: North Mankato, Minnesota : Picture Window Books, [2021] | Series: Astrid and Apollo | Audience: Ages 6-8. | Audience: Grades K-1. | Summary: During their trip to the farm, Astrid and Apollo enjoy Grandma's funny stories and Uncle Meng's magic tricks while picking vegetables to sell at the farmers' market. Includes facts about the Hmong.
Identifiers: LCCN 2021002463 (print) | LCCN 2021002464 (ebook) | ISBN 9781515882077 (hardcover) | ISBN 9781515883173 (paperback) | ISBN 9781515891741 (ebook pdf)
Subjects: CYAC: Twins—Fiction. | Brothers and sisters—Fiction. | Grandmothers—Fiction. | Uncles—Fiction. | Gardens—Fiction. | Hmong Americans—Fiction.
Classification: LCC PZ7.1.B5333 Ap 2021 (print) | LCC PZ7.1.B5333 (ebook) | DDC [E]—dc23
LC record available at https://lccn.loc.gov/2021002463
LC ebook record available at https://lccn.loc.gov/20210024

Designer: Kay Fraser

Design Elements: Shutterstock: Ingo Menhard, 60, Yangxiong (pattern), 5 and throughout

Printed and bound in the USA. 4270

Table of Contents

Hi, I'm Astrid. My twin brother is Apollo, and we were born in Minnesota. We live here with our mom, dad, and little sister, Eliana.

ASTRID GAO NOU

Hi, I'm Apollo! Our mom and dad were both born in Laos. They came to the United States when they were very young and grew up here.

APOLLO NOU KOU

MOM, DAD, AND ELIANA GAO CHEE

HMONG WORDS

dee (DEE)—cucumber. Hmong spelling: *dib*

dee lia (DEE lee-YAH)—watermelon. Hmong spelling: *dib liab*

Gao Chee (GOW chee)—shiny girl. Hmong spelling: *Nkauj Ci*

Gao Hlee (GOW lee)—moon girl. Hmong spelling: *Nkauj Hlis*

Gao Nou (GOW new)—sun girl. Hmong spelling: *Nkauj Hnub*

gao (GOW)—girl; it is often placed in front of a girl's name. Hmong spelling: *nkauj*

Hmong (MONG)—a group of people who came to the U.S. from Laos. Many Hmong from Laos now live in Minnesota. Hmong spelling: *Hmoob*

karr (KAW-er)—a bamboo basket with straps that is worn on a person's back. Hmong spelling: *kawm*

lay (LAY)—a woven mat from Southeast Asia. Hmong spelling: *lev*

naw maw (NAW maw)—to eat. Hmong spelling: *noj mov*

Nia Thy (nee-YAH thy)—grandmother on the mother's side. Hmong spelling: *Niam Tais*

Nou Kou (NEW koo)—star. Hmong spelling: *Hnub Qub*

tou (TOO)—boy or son; it is often placed in front of a boy's name. Hmong spelling: *tub*

CHAPTER 1

Nia Thy Is Here!

Eliana was sitting next to Astrid and Apollo outside their house. She pointed at a blue van driving down the street. "Nia Thy!" she said.

"It's Uncle Meng's van," said Apollo.

"Eliana, you were right!" said Astrid.

Mom and Dad came out of the house. "Yes, Grandma and Uncle Meng are visiting today," said Mom.

"They're bringing fruits and vegetables from Grandma's farm," Dad said.

Eliana said, "Nia Thy is here!"

Everyone waited as Uncle Meng parked in the driveway.

"Hi, Uncle Meng!" Apollo walked over to the van. Astrid and Eliana followed him.

"Hi!" said Uncle Meng as he stepped out of the van.

Grandma stepped out of the other side.

"Grandma, we missed you!" said Astrid.

"Hi, Grandma!" said Apollo.

Eliana ran up to Grandma. "Hi, Nia Thy!"

Grandma hugged the kids. "Nia Thy missed you too! Even if I just saw you last week," said Grandma.

Uncle Meng opened the van's side door. A cucumber dropped onto the ground.

"Coo-coo-ber!" said Eliana.

Apollo picked up the cucumber.

"Here's more!" Uncle Meng reached in the van and took out a large paper bag. "Grandma and I picked them today."

"Are they for the farmers market?" Mom asked.

Uncle Meng gave Dad the bag. "These ones are for you to eat."

Dad looked in the bag. "This is a lot of cucumbers!"

Uncle Meng nodded. "We still have a big field of cucumbers left. Kids, want to help us pick them tomorrow? We'll be selling them at the farmers market on Saturday."

"Oh, I love going to the farmers market! And I want to visit Grandma's farm!" said Astrid.

"Me too!" Apollo said.

"That's a great idea," said Dad.

Mom agreed. "I like that. Now let's go inside and taste these cucumbers!"

As they walked into the house, Uncle Meng said, "I call the farmers market the *magic* market. What we sell there grew from a seed, like magic! Wait, what's that?"

He leaned down and put his hand next to Eliana's ear. He pulled out a coin and said, "Ta-da! See? Magic!"

"Wow!" said Eliana. She stared at the coin and everyone laughed.

* * *

The next day, Uncle Meng and Grandma arrived early to pick up the twins. Mom and Dad walked them outside.

"Have fun!" said Dad.

"Remember to wear your hats and sunscreen. Also, ask Grandma to tell you stories," said Mom.

Astrid and Apollo nodded and climbed into the van.

"Good morning, you two!" Uncle Meng said.

"Good morning." Astrid and Apollo both yawned.

Grandma smiled from the front seat. "My little Gao Nou and Nou Kou are so tired. You can sleep. It's a long drive to the farm."

The twins slept the whole way. They didn't wake up until the van went over big bumps in the dirt road.

"Sorry. The road here is very bumpy," said Uncle Meng.

Apollo looked out the window. "This farm is huge!" he said.

Outside were large green fields. Each field had tall and small plants. Thick stems and leaves grew around them. People were already in the fields, picking fruits and vegetables.

"Which part is Grandma's?"
Astrid asked.

"Grandma's garden is right there.
It's near that little tree," said Uncle
Meng. He parked on the grass by
the tree.

Astrid and Apollo got out of the van.

Grandma handed them big baskets. "These are for cucumbers," she said.

Then Grandma put a karr, a Hmong basket with straps, on her back. Next she put on her big straw hat.

Astrid and Apollo rubbed sunscreen on their faces and arms. Then they put on their hats. Astrid had a floppy pink gardening hat. Apollo wore Dad's old blue fishing hat.

Uncle Meng smiled and gave them gloves. "You kids look ready to work in your hats."

"We don't want to get sunburned," said Astrid.

"That's smart," said Uncle Meng. He put on his baseball cap.

Grandma pointed to the field. "See the cucumbers? We pick from these rows here. When we're done, we'll pick watermelons over there," she said.

Astrid and Apollo looked at the rows of cucumbers. Wooden poles stood between the plants. Leaves and vines twisted up the poles.

Then Apollo said, "I see a cucumber!"

CHAPTER 2

Uncle Meng's Mystery

Apollo pointed to a little cucumber hanging near a big leaf.

Astrid smiled. "It looks like a pickle."

"That one's not ready yet. Find the long ones. Don't pull them off. Use these to cut the stem," said Uncle Meng. He gave them garden scissors.

"Thanks," said Astrid and Apollo.

Uncle Meng pointed all around.

"Can you feel the magic here?" he asked. "Now you two help Grandma pick cucumbers. I'll go pick green beans." He walked to the other side of the farm.

The twins followed Grandma.

"Uncle Meng likes talking about magic," said Apollo.

"It *is* magical if you think how everything here came from little seeds," Astrid said.

Apollo shrugged. "I guess. Grandma, how do we know which cucumbers to pick?"

"Look for ones that are six to seven inches long," said Grandma. She held her hands out to show them. "Make sure it's dark green all over."

Astrid saw a yellow cucumber. "What about yellow?"

"Yellow means it's too old. It won't taste good. It should be a nice green color," said Grandma.

"Like this?" Apollo showed Grandma a pretty green cucumber.

"Yes. Now press on it. If it's hard, it's ready. If it's soft, it's no good," said Grandma.

Apollo pressed down. "It feels hard. I think it's ready."

Grandma took out her scissors. "We cut it off near the top. You don't want to break the stem or no more cucumbers will grow from it." She cut the cucumber and put it in Apollo's basket.

"Thanks, Grandma," said Apollo.

Astrid watched them and smiled. It was nice and quiet on the farm. The sun was hot, but she had shade from her floppy hat. Warm breezes blew by. The leaves on the plants moved in the wind. The air smelled clean.

"It's peaceful here, Grandma. Is that why you like farming?" asked Astrid.

Grandma walked between the rows of cucumbers. "It reminds me of when I was a little girl. In Laos, I helped my grandmother on her farm every day."

"What was that like?" asked Apollo.

Uncle Meng waved.

When they ran out of baskets
again, Apollo went to get more. This
time Uncle Meng was on another side
of the farm. He looked like he was
trying to find something in the leaves.

"Hi, Uncle Meng!" Apollo said.

Uncle Meng waved again.

What is he doing? Apollo
wondered.

"I feel like Uncle Meng is looking for something," Apollo said to Astrid when he got back.

"I thought that too!" said Astrid. "But what?"

"I don't know," said Apollo.

"Maybe he's just picking leaves. But I'm not sure why he would do that," said Astrid.

"We have to figure out what he is doing," said Apollo.

"Hurry, kids," called Grandma.

They moved along and picked more cucumbers.

"Maybe he's looking for bugs?" said Astrid.

"Or worms?" Apollo said.

"Look!" Astrid said, pointing.

CHAPTER 3

The Red Pepper

Astrid and Apollo got a water bottle and soap from the van. They washed their hands while Grandma put a colorful mat under the tree.

"Sit on this. It's called a lay. In Laos we sat on these all the time," she said.

Astrid and Apollo sat next to Grandma. She opened the bags of lunch Mom had packed for them. She set the food out on the lay.

Uncle Meng unfolded a fishing chair. He put it by the back of the van. He sat down and stretched out his legs.

"Uncle Meng, don't you want to eat lunch with us?" Astrid asked.

He showed them a banana peel. "Thanks. I already ate. I'm taking a nap now," he said. He put his baseball cap over his face and closed his eyes.

Grandma laughed. "The sun makes Uncle Meng sleepy," she said.

Astrid and Apollo looked at him. He was already asleep!

"Naw maw. Eat," said Grandma. She gave them sticky rice. Then she unwrapped a pack of beef jerky.

"There's a spicy one and a sweet one," Grandma said.

"Is it the beef jerky from the Hmong restaurant?" asked Apollo.

"Yes, your mom told me she bought it yesterday," Grandma said.

Apollo bit into the chewy beef. "This spicy one is the best!"

Astrid took a bite of hers. "I got the yummy sweet one!"

"Drink water and have corn," said Grandma. She gave them water and corn on the cob.

Astrid ate the corn. "This corn is good!"

Grandma pointed at the fields. "Hmong farmers grow corn here too," she said.

Astrid and Apollo saw the other farmers still picking fruits and vegetables. Their big hats moved up and down as they worked.

A breeze blew past them. Nearby, Uncle Meng was snoring softly. The sun was hot. It was very quiet. Astrid and Apollo felt calm and happy.

Apollo sat back and rubbed his stomach. "That was a great lunch."

Grandma peeled an orange and passed out slices. "Eat these. They're as sweet as sugar."

Apollo ate a slice of orange and said, "Grandma, can you tell us another story from when you were little?"

"We want to hear more!" said Astrid.

Grandma smiled. "One time I saw a giant watermelon at the farm."

"How big was it?" asked Apollo.

"It was the biggest, fattest one I ever saw!" she said. "My grandmother helped me cut it from the stem. But when I tried to pick it up, it was too big!"

"What happened?" Apollo asked.

"I dropped it!" Grandma said.

"Did it break?" asked Astrid.

Grandma laughed. "It didn't break. But it rolled down the hill!"

"Oh no!" Astrid said. She pictured Grandma chasing a watermelon down a hill.

Apollo thought of Grandma looking everywhere for it. "Did you find it?" he asked.

Grandma shook her head. "When we got to the bottom of the hill, it was gone!" she said. "We went to every village. We asked everyone, 'Did you see a big watermelon roll by?'"

"And what did they say?" asked Apollo.

Grandma shrugged. "No one had seen it. My grandmother said maybe it rolled all the way to Vietnam. Or maybe up to China. Maybe it's still rolling today!"

Astrid and Apollo laughed. Grandma laughed too.

"When we got home, no one believed I had found the biggest watermelon. But my grandmother didn't scold me." Grandma said.

"I love that story," said Astrid.

"So do I. Please tell us another one!" said Apollo.

Grandma pointed at Uncle Meng. "I can tell you about why Uncle Meng loves magic."

Apollo sat up. "Why?"

Grandma spoke softly. "Uncle Meng helps me pick vegetables, but he is always looking for something else."

"I saw him do that when he was picking green beans!" said Astrid.

"Me too, Grandma!" said Apollo. "At first I thought he was looking for beans. But he looked like he was really trying to find another thing."

Grandma put a finger to her lips.

"Uncle Meng is shy about it. But he wants to find a special pepper!"

Astrid thought of Uncle Meng always talking about magic. "A *magic* pepper?" she asked.

"Yes," said Grandma. "When Uncle Meng was little, he read a story about a boy and magic beans. He didn't like beans, but he liked peppers. So he wished to find a long, red pepper. He said that could be like a magic bean."

"You mean the pepper could make a big pepper plant? Like a giant beanstalk?" Apollo asked.

Grandma nodded.

"Does he really believe that?" Astrid asked.

Grandma smiled. "He did when he was a little boy. Uncle Meng is a man now, but sometimes, he still looks for the red pepper, just for fun."

"Why doesn't he look for it when picking peppers?" said Apollo.

"Yes, why look for it with the beans?" asked Astrid.

Grandma laughed. "So many questions! Uncle Meng said the magic red pepper might grow anywhere, not just with peppers. So he looks for it everywhere."

"What does the pepper look like?" said Apollo.

"It's long and bright red," said Grandma.

"That's a fun story!" Astrid smiled at Apollo. He smiled back.

Grandma stood up. "Now it's time to get back to work. Come, let's go pick watermelons."

Astrid and Apollo stood up too.

Grandma looked at Uncle Meng. "Meng, time to wake up!"

CHAPTER 4

Thump-Thump

Uncle Meng shook in his chair and woke up.

Astrid and Apollo helped Grandma fold the lay and pack up the lunch.

Uncle Meng stood up and stretched. He opened the van and showed them a big wagon in the back.

"This is for watermelons," he said.

Apollo helped Uncle Meng lift the wagon from the van. Apollo really wanted to ask him about the magic pepper, but he didn't.

As they walked toward the field of watermelons, Astrid smiled. She liked thinking about Uncle Meng wishing for a magic pepper. And she liked thinking about Grandma as a little girl gardening on a hill.

Apollo was smiling too. He whispered, "I wonder where that magic red pepper is. And I wonder what happened to that big watermelon!"

Soon they got to the field. Watermelons were everywhere!

Grandma said, "If you find a watermelon that's too heavy, tell your uncle. He'll help you put it in the wagon."

"How do we know it's ready to pick?" asked Astrid.

Uncle Meng pointed to a big watermelon on the ground. "See this curly part sticking out of the stem? Make sure it's brown. Also look for a flat yellow spot on the bottom." He showed them the spot.

"I see it!" said Apollo.

"Now tap on the watermelon. Listen for a sound like a knock on the door." Uncle Meng tapped on it and said, "Hear that?"

Astrid and Apollo heard *thump-thump!* They nodded.

"This one's ready," said Uncle Meng.

Apollo saw a round watermelon nearby.

The curly top of the stem looked brown. He turned the heavy melon over to find the flat yellow spot. Then he tapped the watermelon.

"I hear the sound!" Apollo said.

Uncle Meng checked it and said, "Good job!"

Next Astrid tried to find one. She saw a large watermelon next to a small one. She looked for the brown part of the stem. She found the yellow spot. She tapped the watermelon and said, "Here's another one!"

Uncle Meng looked at it. "You got it!" he said.

That afternoon, Astrid and Apollo walked all over the field. They looked for brown curly stems and yellow spots. They tapped the melons and listened for the *thump-thump* sound. Then they filled the wagon with many, many watermelons.

Every time they saw Uncle Meng checking under the leaves, they grinned.

"I wish we could find a red pepper for Uncle Meng," Astrid whispered.

"That would be cool!" said Apollo.

When they were finally done picking watermelons, they helped Uncle Meng wheel the wagon back to the van.

"We picked so many watermelons and cucumbers today," said Apollo.

"We will have many to sell at the market tomorrow!" said Grandma.

CHAPTER 5

Magic Melon

The next morning, the whole family met Grandma and Uncle Meng at the farmers market.

Dad parked next to Uncle Meng's van. He helped him set up a big tent for shade. Apollo helped Mom put up a long table. Astrid and Grandma went to the van to get the cucumbers.

Eliana sat in her stroller. She watched everyone get ready.

Astrid put little baskets of cucumbers on the table. Uncle Meng rolled the wagon with watermelons to the front of the table. Apollo and Dad carried the green beans to put on the table too.

The market was bright and colorful. The air felt hot. Cars drove past on the busy street nearby. It was noisy out. Soon customers came. Everyone was excited to look at the fresh fruits and vegetables.

Astrid and Apollo looked at the other tables. They saw farmers selling purple eggplants and small green Thai eggplants. They saw tables with big white onions and bright orange carrots.

They saw tables with lemongrass, red tomatoes, and sweet yellow corn.

Customers stopped at Grandma's table. One man bought two baskets of cucumbers for his kids and grandchildren. A woman picked five bags of green beans for her restaurant. A family wanted three of the biggest watermelons for a picnic.

Astrid and Apollo helped Grandma as more people lined up. The customers liked everything on the table.

After they left, Apollo said, "People are buying a lot!"

"I'm sure they are. Kids, did you hear about Grandma's watermelon that rolled away?" said Mom.

"Yes, and it's still rolling today!" Astrid and Apollo said.

"Maybe it was a magic melon!" said Uncle Meng.

Just then a woman walked by carrying a bag of red peppers.

Astrid turned to Apollo. "I have an idea!"

"I think I know what it is!" Apollo said.

"Mom, can we look at other tables?" Astrid asked.

"Yes, but don't go far," said Mom.

Astrid and Apollo walked around the market until they saw it.

A Hmong farmer was selling packs of hot peppers. He had round bell peppers and skinny chili peppers. He had short, spicy peppers and long, curly peppers.

Apollo said, "Look!"

"I see it!" said Astrid.

They bought a pack and hurried back to Grandma's table. Then Apollo gave Eliana something. Astrid whispered to her.

Eliana held her arm behind her back. She walked up to Uncle Meng and put her hand behind his ear.

"Dah-dah!" she said and pulled out a long red pepper.

"Wow!" said Uncle Meng in surprise. "It *is* magic!"

Everybody laughed. Grandma looked over at Astrid and Apollo and smiled.

- Hmong people first lived in southern China. Many of them moved to Southeast Asia in the 1800s. Some Hmong decided to stay in the country of Laos (pronounced *LAH-ohs*).

LAOS

- In the 1950s, a war called the Vietnam War started in Southeast Asia. The United States joined this war. They asked the Hmong in Laos to help them. When the U.S. lost the war, Hmong people had to leave Laos.

- After 1975, many Hmong came to the U.S. as refugees. Refugees are people who escape from their country to find a new, safe place to live. Today, Minnesota is home to around 85,000 Hmong.

- Many Hmong American families enjoy outdoor activities like camping, boating, and fishing.

MORE ABOUT
HMONG FARMERS

- In Laos, Hmong people lived in the mountains and not on flat land. Because of this, many Hmong farmers used the land on the hillsides to farm.

- Many Hmong people carried their crops on their backs using a karr, a Hmong basket. Today some Hmong farmers still use these baskets.

- Hmong American farmers make up more than half of the farmers at the farmers markets in the Twin Cities in Minnesota.

- Often many members of one family may help at the farm. This means grandparents and grandchildren can work together to pick fruits and vegetables, just like Astrid and Apollo did with their grandmother!

- Some fruits and vegetables that Hmong farmers sell at the farmers market include snow peas, long green beans, cucumbers, bitter melon, tomatoes, cilantro, corn, and spicy red peppers called Hmong peppers!

GLOSSARY

beef jerky (BEEF JUR-kee)—meat that has been cut into strips and dried

cucumber (KYOO-kuhm-bur)—a long, green vegetable that grows on a vine and has a lot of seeds

customer (KUHS-tuh-muhr)—a person who buys goods or services

eggplant (EG-plant)—a purple vegetable with white flesh and tiny seeds

farmers market (FAHR-murz MAHR-kit)—a gathering of people for the purpose of buying or selling goods such as vegetables and fruits

lemongrass (LEM-uhn-gras)—a grass that smells like lemons and is used as a seasoning

picnic (PIK-nik)—a meal that is eaten outside, often at a park

scold (SKOHLD)—to tell someone in an angry way that he or she has done something wrong

sunscreen (SUHN-skreen)—a lotion that protects your skin from the sun

Vietnam (vee-et-NAHM)—a country in southeastern Asia

watermelon (WAW-tur-mel-uhn)—a large, juicy fruit that grows on vines

1. Astrid and Apollo helped Grandma pick cucumbers and watermelons at the farm. Have you ever picked fruits or vegetables from a garden or farm before? Share what that was like.

2. Grandma said farming in Laos is different than in the U.S. How? What did Astrid think about when Grandma said that?

3. Why did Uncle Meng want to find a red pepper? What story made him think a pepper could be magic?

1. What happened to the big watermelon Grandma picked when she was a little girl? Draw a picture of Grandma chasing it.

2. Uncle Meng told Astrid and Apollo to check for three things when looking for a good watermelon. Make a list of the things he said they should look for.

3. Astrid and Apollo saw different kinds of fruits and vegetables at the farmers market. Write a paragraph about the fruits and vegetables you see at the market.

ABOUT THE AUTHOR

V.T. Bidania has been writing stories ever since she was five years old. She was born in Laos and grew up in St. Paul, Minnesota, right where Astrid and Apollo live! She has an MFA in creative writing from The New School and is a McKnight Writing Fellow. She lives outside of the Twin Cities and spends her free time reading all the books she can find, writing more stories, and playing with her family's sweet Morkie.

ABOUT THE ILLUSTRATOR

Evelt Yanait is a freelance children's digital artist from Barcelona, Spain, where she grew up drawing and reading wonderful illustrated books. After working as a journalist for an NGO for many years, she decided to focus on illustration, her true passion. She loves to learn, write, travel, and watch documentaries, discovering and capturing new lifestyles and stories whenever she can. She also does social work with children and youth, and she's currently earning a Social Education degree.